Clifford's Puppy days ™

GRADUATION DAY

By Danielle Denega
Illustrated by Jay Johnson

ISBN-13: 978-0-439-90900-6
ISBN-10: 0-439-90900-7

30 29 28 27 26 25 24 23 22   40   17/0

Designed by Michael Massen
Printed in the U.S.A.
First printing, May 2007

SCHOLASTIC INC.

New York   Toronto   London   Auckland   Sydney
Mexico City   New Delhi   Hong Kong   Buenos Aires

P9-DDR-449

The Howard family loved their little red puppy.
But Clifford was making mischief.
Clifford tried to run away in the park.
Then Clifford sneaked food from the table.

Clifford knocked over the trash can and chewed up Mr. Howard's best shoes!

Emily Elizabeth told Clifford, "You need to go to puppy school!"

Clifford was worried at first, but puppy school was fun!
When the puppy trainer told Clifford to sit, Clifford
rolled around on his back.

"Down," the puppy trainer said to Clifford. But Clifford tore up the grass.

"Come," the puppy trainer called to Clifford. He chased a butterfly instead.
Clifford was not a very good student.

"Clifford needs practice," Mr. Howard explained to Emily Elizabeth. "Can you help him?"

"Will I have time to learn my words for the spelling bee *and* help Clifford with his puppy school commands?" Emily Elizabeth wondered.

"Many of your spelling words are the same commands Clifford has to learn," Mrs. Howard said, holding up one of Emily Elizabeth's flash cards. "Maybe you and Clifford could help each other."

"That's a great idea!" Emily Elizabeth said.

"Okay, Clifford. You are going to graduate from puppy school. And I am going to win my school spelling bee," Emily Elizabeth said. "But we have to work together!"

Emily Elizabeth read her first flash card aloud, "Sit. S-I-T."
Then she showed Clifford how to sit. And he sat.
"Good boy, Clifford," Emily Elizabeth said.

Emily Elizabeth read another flash card, "Down. D-O-W-N."
Then she showed Clifford how to lie down. And he did it.

"Great job!" Emily Elizabeth shouted.

This time, when the puppy trainer told Clifford to sit, he sat right at her feet.

When the puppy trainer said, "Down," Clifford lay down on his belly.

Puppy School
Graduate
Clifford

Clifford looked at Emily Elizabeth and wagged his tail.
He would graduate from puppy school after all!

Emily Elizabeth was so proud of Clifford, but she was still nervous about her spelling bee.

She didn't need to worry. With Clifford's help, she had learned all her words and won!

"Thank you, Clifford. I couldn't have done it without you," Emily Elizabeth whispered.

Clifford licked her nose and thought the same thing.